The Shelf Elf

Jackie Mims Hopkins

Illustrated by Rebecca McKillip Thornburgh

Fort Atkinson, Wisconsin

Published by UpstartBooks
W5527 Highway 106
P.O. Box 800
Fort Atkinson, Wisconsin 53538-0800
1-800-448-4887

Text © 2004 by Jackie Mims Hopkins
Illustrations © 2004 by Rebecca Thornburgh

The paper used in this publication meets the minimum requirements of American National Standard for Information Science — Permanence of Paper for Printed Library Material. ANSI/NISO Z39.48.

In loving memory of Susan Kelley, library coordinator of Cypress Fairbanks Independent School District.

Thank you to Pat Miller, Aileen Kirkham, and Bobbie McDonald for all of their creative Shelf Elf contributions.
Thank you also to Jane Rothe, the best library assistant ever.

—J.M.H.

For my sister Emily, prodigiously omnivorous reader.
—R.McK.T.

By the candlelight,
the shoemaker and his wife
watched the two little elves
dance merrily out of sight.

The End

 id you ever wonder what became of those elves after they left the shoemaker's shop?

I can tell you, because I am one of them.

My name is Skoob, and the other elf was Skeeter. Skeeter went up north to work with his cousin, a toy maker, and I danced right off the page and into this library.

ow that I live in the library, I have a new job. I'm a shelf elf.

I take care of the books and the library shelves.

Stacks, also known as the Grand Dewey Daddy shelf elf, gave me a book with helpful tips on library manners and book care.

 tacks told me about a special award that is given to shelf elves.

It is called the Golden Shelf Elf Award.

I am trying to earn it by taking good care of books, and keeping the shelves straight.

He also told me that the library has to have girls and boys with nice library manners.

Some of the things he told me to look for are children who use shelf markers, quiet voices, and walking feet.

Maybe you can help me win the Golden Shelf Elf Award and we can share it.

ne of the tools I use in my new job is a shelf marker. Let's look in my book to find out more about using shelf markers.

Use a shelf marker, you can't go wrong,
put books back where they belong.

The shelf marker holds my place on the shelf while I decide if I want to check the book out. If I don't want the book, the shelf marker shows me where the book belongs.

Come on, let's find a book to check out.

ook at these shelves.

Can you find the three books that weren't put back
on the shelves correctly?

I'll give you a hint: books should be standing
tall on the shelf with their spines showing.
That way, everyone can read the titles and see
the call numbers at the bottom of the spines.

his one looks interesting. I would like to keep it for a long time. I wonder if it would be okay to check it out for a whole year?

Let's see what my Shelf Elf's Guide says about this.

Return your books when they are due, so others can enjoy them, too.

Keeping a book for a year wouldn't be fair. Everyone should return books on time so others can check them out.

his book is making me hungry. I think I'll eat a little snack and have some juice while I read it.

Before I get my snack, I better find out if there is a rule about eating and drinking while reading a book.

Keep your books clean and neat,
away from all you drink and eat.

Everyone should have clean hands when they look at books. Food could stain the pages and if the juice spills, it would make the pages wet.

Remember to keep books away from anything wet.

ook, the corner of this page is bent down. Someone must have been marking the place before finishing the book. I think I remember reading something about this in my guidebook. It's called "dog-earing." A bookmark should be used to save your place.

If you need to save your place,
stick a bookmark in that space.

If you don't have a bookmark, just put a piece of paper between the pages where you stopped reading.

This page is torn.

Someone must have turned the page too quickly.
It was probably an accident, but we have to
remember to turn the pages carefully.

Turn the pages with great care;
leave them whole without a tear.

h no, this page has been scribbled and chewed on.

This book wasn't kept in a safe place. A baby sister or brother may have colored on the pages.

It's important to keep books in a place where younger children and pets can't get them.

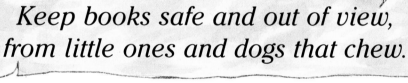

Keep books safe and out of view,
from little ones and dogs that chew.

 he librarian, Ms. Paige Turner, needs to know about the problems in this book.

Sometimes she and Stacks can repair the books.

I'll put it in the book hospital box and maybe they will teach me how to repair books too.

 hank you for helping me today.

With helpful girls and boys like you, we will surely earn the Golden Shelf Elf Award someday!

It's time to say good-bye, but please remember to whisper in your quiet library voice. Loud noises hurt my tiny ears.

When in the library make this choice: always use your quiet voice.

Goodnight, Little Gremlin
Twilight Tales
One More Moonbeam
READ
READ!
S E
F NAR
F NEN
F NIN

Remember your friend Skoob whenever you visit the library!

You may not see him, but you can be sure the Shelf Elf is around somewhere—and working hard to get that award!

The library is filled with amazing things—books! In books you can find science, history, adventure, mystery, magic, and fun. There are some amazing things in this book, too. See if you can find:

an alien spaceship

a biplane

a birdcage

a bird's nest with eggs

blackbirds in a pie

a broom with a bucket

a bucket on a rope

a cactus

two clotheslines

a covered wagon

a dinosaur

a dish and spoon

a fishbowl

ten frogs!

a girl on a swing

a hammock

a hot air balloon

a jack-o'-lantern

Jack on his beanstalk

a juggler on a unicycle

a key

a kite

two ladders

a mailbox

a man fishing

a man playing a banjo

Mary, Mary, Quite Contrary

a mermaid

a mouse pilot

a paper airplane

a pendulum clock

a piano keyboard

a pirate

a playing card painter

a porthole

a portrait of a lady

Puss in Boots

Rapunzel's Tower

a sea serpent

a sleeping kitty cat

a smiling school bus

a snowman

a stop sign

two suitcases

a teacup

a telescope

a tent

Three Blind Mice

a three-masted schooner

a tiger tail

a train

a treasure chest

a treasure map

a whale

the White Rabbit

windows and doors (lots!)